CHL

jFIC R763wi
Rounds, Glen, 1906-
Wild Appaloosa /

W9-BWW-690

ESLC90

Children's

DENVER
PUBLIC LIBRARY

FINE FOR OVERTIME

DEMCO

DATE DUE
12 8 89

RO1134 17908

Holiday House Books
Written and Illustrated by Glen Rounds

OL' PAUL, THE MIGHTY LOGGER

LUMBERCAMP

PAY DIRT

THE BLIND COLT

STOLEN PONY

RODEO

WHITEY AND THE RUSTLERS

HUNTED HORSES

WHITEY AND THE BLIZZARD

BUFFALO HARVEST

LONE MUSKRAT

WHITEY TAKES A TRIP

WHITEY ROPES AND RIDES

WHITEY AND THE WILD HORSE

WHISTLEPUNK OF CAMP 15

WHITEY'S FIRST ROUNDUP

WILD ORPHAN

WHITEY AND THE COLT-KILLER

WHITEY'S NEW SADDLE

THE TREELESS PLAINS

THE PRAIRIE SCHOONERS

WILD HORSES OF THE RED DESERT

ONCE WE HAD A HORSE

THE COWBOY TRADE

THE DAY THE CIRCUS CAME TO LONE TREE

WILDLIFE AT YOUR DOORSTEP

MR. YOWDER AND THE LION ROAR CAPSULES

THE BEAVER: HOW HE WORKS

MR. YOWDER AND THE STEAMBOAT

MR. YOWDER AND THE GIANT BULL SNAKE

MR. YOWDER, THE PERIPATETIC SIGN PAINTER:
    THREE TALL TALES

BLIND OUTLAW

MR. YOWDER AND THE TRAIN ROBBERS

WILD
APPALOOSA

WILD
APPALOOSA

WRITTEN AND ILLUSTRATED BY

Glen Rounds

Holiday House, New York

DENVER
PUBLIC LIBRARY

FEB - - 1984

CITY & COUNTY OF DENVER

R01134 17908

Copyright © 1983 by Glen Rounds
All rights reserved
Printed in the United States of America
First Edition

Library of Congress Cataloging in Publication Data
Rounds, Glen, 1906–
   Wild Appaloosa.

   Summary: A handsome, wild Appaloosa filly, desired
by wild horse hunters, makes a young boy's dream come
true.
   1. Horses—Juvenile fiction.   [1. Horses—Fiction]
I. Title.
PZ10.3.R76Whl   1983   [Fic]   82-48751
ISBN 0-8234-0482-X

jFIC R763wi
Rounds, Glen, 1906-
Wild Appaloosa /

For CARRIE, *this tale from*
The Treeless Plains

In the West the legend of the magnificent wild horse, usually a great stallion—either white or jet black—still persists. Even today, in bunkhouses and ranches on the High Plains, there are men and boys who dream of becoming famous by capturing and taming such a horse for their own personal use.

Nearly all of those extraordinary horses existed only in the old tales, or in men's imaginations. But it is true that once in a long, long time such an unusual horse did show up among the stunted wild ones.

And it happened that not so many years ago, word spread across the range that a truly showy Appaloosa yearling had been seen a time or two with a small band of wild horses, far back in the Badlands.

As it turned out, this was not one of the legendary stallions but, instead, a beautifully marked yearling filly. And this story of her escape from the wild horse hunters and of her adventures afterwards may or may not be entirely true. But it could well have been.

WILD
APPALOOSA

1

THE EARLY MORNING sun was warm on the backs of the twenty or thirty wild horses grazing over the little flat in the highest, roughest part of the Badlands. The last of the winter's snow had melted even on the north slopes, and now the horses nosed among the dry brown tussocks in a greedy search for the tender shoots of new spring grass that were just beginning to appear.

At one time there had been great herds of wild horses such as these scattered all up and

down what are called the High Plains. But they were mostly small and of little value, so as the country settled up, the ranchers, wanting the grass and water for their own livestock, had set out to clear them from the range. Over the years hundreds had been simply rounded up and shot, while others were shipped by the trainload to the meat-packers in the East.

So now there was only this one small band left. To escape the wild horse hunters, they had left the open country and moved deep into the Badlands, a hundred-mile-square maze of high rocky ridges, deep twisting canyons, and great wind-worn buttes.

The grass in this space was sparse, and grew in widely scattered spots while the few water holes and springs were often miles apart. So to survive, these horses were forced to travel long distances each day in their search for grass and water.

However, it was a place where men seldom came, and there were few wolves or even mountain lions to threaten them. In winter the bitter

cold and deep snows took a certain toll of the weaker horses, and falls or rock slides accounted for the death of some others. But in time they had adapted themselves to life in those harsh surroundings.

Like most wild horses, these were small and tough and scruffy looking compared to the larger and better-fed range horses belonging to the ranchers. Their colors ranged from faded browns and bays to rusty black, mouse color or clay-bank gray. Their manes and tails were long, matted with burrs and mud—and the edges of their untrimmed hooves were broken and rough from wear on the rocky plains.

But there was one yearling among them, a long-legged, high-headed filly that stood out from the rest, both because of her size and her coloring. She was already larger than any of the other last year's colts, and besides that, she wore the striking Appaloosa markings.

Her overall color was a deep bluish steel gray, but a great patch of white, dappled with egg-sized dark spots, covered her entire rump, blending into the darker color down the sides. Another patch of white, edged with hundreds of darker speckles, covered her forehead and the pink skin of her muzzle.

Her ears were sharp and alert, while her head was more delicately shaped than those of the other wild horses. Another striking feature was her one pale blue eye—what is called in that country a "china eye." This was simply a matter of coloring and had no effect on her seeing, but did add to her already outstanding appearance.

Altogether, this filly showed promise of growing into the sort of wild horse every man and boy in that country dreamed of some day capturing and taming.

Her mother, a dun-colored mare with the black mustang stripe down her backbone, already had a new spring colt following her, and the little Appaloosa had been weaned long ago. But she still spent much of her time near the old mare.

Now while the older horses searched for the new green grass and the nursing colts butted their mothers' flanks, the Appaloosa and the other yearlings left off their own grazing now and again to race about or engage in mock battles with one another.

There was no wind, and as the sun warmed their hiding places under the grass, the big blue flies wakened and began to buzz about their morning's business. But except for that, or a horse occasionally clearing his nostrils, the only sound to be heard was the faint far-off quarreling of magpies.

Yet peaceful as this high place appeared to be, the older horses seemed uneasy, interrupting their grazing every few moments to throw up their heads and look about, listening and sniffing the air. And every little while one or another of the older mares would leave the others and climb to the top of some bit of higher ground for a look around.

During the years since they'd drifted up into the Badlands, these horses had seldom been troubled by either ranchers or wild horse hunters. But in the last week or two, they'd several

times seen riders skylined on distant ridges.

The wild horses were as wary of men as the mule deer and antelope that shared the Badlands with them. So even the sight of a far-off horseman was enough to send them moving quietly and quickly down one of the many paths leading deeper into the broken country.

And late one afternoon not long before, as they were cautiously approaching a favorite water hole for their evening drink, the old mare in the lead had caught the scent of men somewhere ahead and heard the unfamiliar ring of iron against stone when a waiting rider's shod horse had stamped its foot to dislodge a fly.

At the old mare's first sharp snort of warning the wild horses had turned back, unseen. And with the mares nipping at their colts to hurry them along, they'd made their way safely by roundabout paths to another watering place miles away.

These unusual happenings had already made the horses uneasy even before they'd first heard the strange new sound that added still more to

their sense of danger.

They'd first heard it one morning, just as they were beginning their day's grazing on another little flat between high ridges. It was a droning sound like nothing they'd ever heard before, and seemed to come from no particular direction. It would grow fainter and louder by turns for a while, then disappear altogether for several hours.

At its faintest, the sound was scarcely louder than the buzzing of the big flies going about their business in the grass. And even at its loudest, it didn't cover the quarreling of magpies in the distance.

But no matter how carefully they looked and listened, the wild horses had not been able to locate the cause of the disturbing sound—and now they heard it for a while each morning, and again in the late afternoon. Like most wild creatures, these horses were distrustful and suspicious of any new thing appearing in their territory, so day by day they were growing more uneasy.

2

ON A ranch across the river, miles from the wild horse range, a man named Torwal and a boy called Bert were fixing a fence when the boy spoke up.

"Look," he said. "There's that airplane circling around again—over there towards the West."

"He's helping the fellows trying to clean that band of wild horses out of the Badlands," Torwal told him. "The horses aren't worth much, but they say there's a real pretty Appaloosa

filly running with them that should be worth a lot of money if they can catch her."

"I'd liked to catch me a wild horse and tame it," Bert remarked. "An Appaloosa would look real nice with my new saddle."

"Maybe so," Torwal said. "But you'd have to catch her first. And those fellows don't seem to be having much luck, so far.

"Those horses have been running back in the Badlands for years," he went on. "They're wild as deer, and know every get-away path and canyon. That's why the horse hunters brought in the man with the airplane to help find them."

"Well," Bert said, "I bet if I had that wild Appaloosa around for a while, I could tame her easy."

"Maybe so," Torwal agreed. "But I doubt you'll ever have a chance. Now let's finish fixing this fence."

Bert said no more. But all morning, as they stretched barbwire and reset fence posts, he thought about somehow catching that Appaloosa horse and taming it himself.

3

W<small>HEN THE</small> horse hunters had first gone into
the Badlands, they thought that it would be an
easy matter to locate the small band of wild
horses and to trap them in one of the many
steep, walled box canyons that are common in
that country.

But they soon discovered that, as Torwal had
told the boy, those horses were wild as deer.
They also found that in that broken country
with its steep ridges and winding canyons, it was

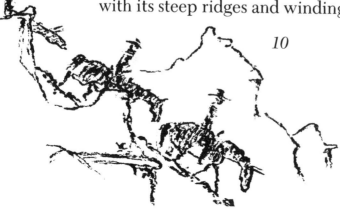

impossible for men on horseback to go directly from one place to another.

They did occasionally catch sight of the wild horses in the distance, but to get near them the men had to ride by long roundabout ways through one crooked canyon after another. Sometimes they found their way blocked by a ridge too steep to climb, or rode deep into a box canyon with no way out except back the way they'd come. And always, by the time they'd found their way to where the horses had been, the entire band would have disappeared. It was a frustrating game of hide-and-seek, and the advantage was all with the horses.

But through their field glasses, they had gotten a glimpse or two of the Appaloosa they wanted so badly to catch. So they'd called in the man with the airplane to help them. Circling high over the Badlands, he had no trouble finding where the horses were grazing each day. However, he always found them close to escape routes that led off in all directions. So there was nothing for the horse hunters to do but wait until the wild band was found near some natural trap.

Then late one afternoon from far off, the man in the airplane saw the horses grazing in a little valley surrounded on three sides by high cliffs. There were only two ways to get in or out of the place. Stock paths ran up and over the low ridges at the valley's head where the cliffs ended. And at the lower end a narrow, steep-walled canyon led down to the rough country below.

The horses had already been to water and seemed to be settling down for the night in what appeared to be a perfect trap. Turning back before the sound of his engine could reach them, the man carried the news to the waiting riders, and they set about making plans for the next day. Before daylight the riders would be in place to block the mouth of the canyon at the bottom of the valley. And as soon as the sun was up, the airplane would fly low to spook the horses away from the paths leading out at the top and drive them down between the high, unclimbable cliffs.

The next morning the wild horses were still in the shallow head of the little valley and had just started their day's feeding when the plane appeared again.

Always before it had been only a tiny speck high in the sky that the horses had never noticed—or perhaps had taken to be a soaring eagle. But this time it appeared without warning, flying low over the top of the nearby ridge. With its engine roaring louder and louder, filling the little valley with an unbelievable sound, it swooped down, straight for the startled horses.

And then another terrible sound was added to the already almost unbearable roar of the plane's engine and the whistle of the wind over its wings. Leaning out of his window with a bullhorn in his hand, the man shouted through the thing. His voice, magnified a hundred times by the horn, echoed back and forth across the valley from cliff to cliff—seeming to come from every side at once.

Terrified by the sight of this strange thing rushing towards them and by the frightening

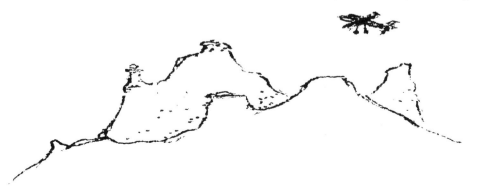

sounds it made, the horses made a rush for the paths leading up the nearest ridge. But before they'd reached the first gentle slope, the plane flew low in front of the leaders and turned them back.

Wheeling, the frightened horses streamed back across the flat towards the paths on the farther slope. But again the plane, circling low, cut off their escape.

Running in blind panic as they tried to get away from this terrible thing that roared back and forth just over their heads, the wild horses swirled first in one direction and in then another through the thickening cloud of dust stirred up by their hooves and the blast from the plane's propeller.

When they heard the plane swooping down on their left, they whirled to the right, and if it roared in front of them, they turned in their tracks and pounded off in a new direction. And the Appaloosa filly ran with the others, her pink nostrils wide and her ears laid flat against her neck.

Little by little the horses were driven into the narrower part of the valley, where the high cliffs hemmed them in on either side, while the plane now flew in lazy circles behind them to prevent their turning back.

With the terrible machine no longer swooping and roaring around and over them, the horses suddenly wheeled and ran straight for the mouth of the unguarded canyon. But just when it seemed they would escape, they found their way barred by the riders who had come up from below, and were forced to turn back again.

As they changed direction, the leaders found themselves facing another narrow opening in the sheer cliff ahead, and without hesitating, the entire band poured through it. But they'd gone only a little way, around a bend or two, when they found they were trapped in a box canyon, with no way out except the way they'd come. And as they turned back, they found the horse hunters again blocking their escape.

When the man in the airplane saw that the wild horses were securely trapped inside the box

canyon, he circled low over the valley a time or two, then flew away.

After building a stout fence of ropes and old logs across the narrowest part of the canyon mouth, the horse hunters remounted and rode slowly around the bend for their first close look at the Appaloosa they'd worked so hard to capture. A horse like that, even as a yearling, would bring them more money than all the rest of the band together.

But no matter how carefully they looked among the frantic horses milling around in the small space at the head of the canyon, they found no sign of the filly.

Disappointed, they watched for a while longer, not wanting to believe that the very horse they'd especially wanted to catch had somehow gotten away. However, they were finally convinced, and unhappily set about getting the rest of the wild horses ready for the trip out of the Badlands.

The colts and yearlings would follow wherever their mothers were driven, but the older

horses had to be caught one by one and roped together in pairs, neck to neck, to make them easier to drive. And some of the more troublesome had to be hobbled by tying their front feet close together. It was a hot dusty business that lasted well into the afternoon before it was finished.

Then leaving one man to guard the fence across the mouth of the trap, the others rode for a while around the valley, still hoping to find some sign of the Appaloosa. But even though they looked in every washout and gully, they found nothing. And there was no way they could read the confused pattern of tracks on tracks made by the horses as they'd been chivied back and forth by the plane.

Meanwhile, huge thunderheads were piling up beyond the ridges, threatening a storm. So in the end the disappointed men gave up the search for the Appaloosa and went off down the lower canyon, driving the hobbled wild horses ahead of them.

4

A FEW DAYS later, on the ranch across the river, Bert and Torwal were fixing the windmill.

"The men brought those wild horses out of the Badlands," Bert remarked, "but the Appaloosa yearling wasn't with them. I wonder what happened to her?"

"The way they tell it," the man answered, "they had the horses trapped in a box canyon, and there was no way she could have gotten away without them seeing.

"Maybe there never was any Appaloosa in the bunch," he went on.

"There had to be," Bert insisted. "The men saw her plain through their field glasses, and so did the man in the airplane when he started chasing them that morning. And they were counting on getting a big price for her."

"Well," Torwal said as he packed grease into the windmill gears, "if the colt was really there, she might have fallen into a washout and been killed while the fellow was trying to chase them into the trap."

"The men said they thought of that," Bert told him. "Said they looked in all those places, and there wasn't any sign of her anywhere. She must have gotten away from them somehow."

"Even if she did get away, like you say," Torwal pointed out, "a colt alone in that country probably wouldn't live very long—there are too many things that might happen to her. Better forget it."

The boy wasn't convinced. "I still bet she did get away," he said. "And I bet she's smart

enough to stay alive."

"Maybe so," the man said, "but now let's us climb down and clean out the tanks."

"I'd still like to go over there and look for her," Bert said after a little. "Being the only horse left in the Badlands, she's probably pretty lonesome. I could leave apples and stuff around for her to find, and I bet she'd get to know me."

"Could be," Torwal answered, "but the Badlands are pretty big, and it'd be like looking for a needle in a haystack, trying to find just one horse hiding out in that rough country."

"I guess you're right," Bert agreed.

But all the way back to the ranch, he thought of the ways he might go about catching that Appaloosa if he could just get a little more time off from his ranch chores.

5

THE MORNING the man in the plane had swooped down on the band of wild horses to drive them into the trap, he had taken careful note of the little Appaloosa grazing with the others.

But as he chivied them this way and that across the flat, circling round them with his wing tip almost in the leaders' faces to turn them away from each possible escape route, their churning back and forth had soon stirred up a great, low-hanging cloud of dust. By then, all the man could see from above were dark, shadowy forms appearing and disappearing in the thickening haze.

So when the horses suddenly wheeled still another time, at the very edge of a deep washout in their path, he didn't see the filly drop from sight as the crumbling bank gave way beneath her feet.

She wasn't hurt by the fall and quickly scrambled up. She could hear the sound of pounding hooves, already some distance off, but the bank was too steep for her to climb. So she simply ran blindly on in the direction she happened to be facing—along the bottom of the twisting gully. She stumbled over rocks and trash left by previous floods, but each time she regained her feet and hurried on. Her only thought was to escape the terrifying sound of the airplane still circling out of sight above the dust cloud.

After some distance, the narrow gully opened

onto a sagebrush flat and an old stock path leading over the ridge at the head of the valley.
Without slowing down, the Appaloosa turned
onto the path and struggled, lunging and slipping, up the steep slope ahead.

Her coat dark with sweat and her breath
coming in harsh, gasping wheezes, she paused
for a moment at the top of the ridge. But hearing
the growl of the plane behind her, she plunged
on down the farther slope.

Paying no attention to where she went, she
simply ran on and on, down steep slopes,
through narrow twisting canyons, and around
great weatherworn buttes. When she could run
no longer, she stopped and stood with her head
down, her trembling legs braced, and her sides
heaving from her exhausted breathing.

For a long time she stood there, while her
sweat-drenched coat dried and her rasping
breathing eased. It was an hour or more before
she moved again. But finally she raised her head
and whinnied a time or two. Flicking her ears

this way and that, she listened for an answer, but when none came she walked stiffly down into a grassy draw nearby, lay down and stretched out on her side.

It was almost dark when the filly was wakened by the sound of thunder and a few heavy drops of cold rain. As the storm rumbled closer, she struggled to her feet and stumbled down the draw to where a wild plum thicket growing against a steep bank offered some shelter from the wind and beating rain:

Some time in the night the rain slacked off and finally stopped altogether. But the filly, shivering from the cold, stayed in her place under the dripping plum bushes until the sky had begun to lighten behind the buttes to the East. Then, when full daylight had come, she came out of the thicket and looked around her.

This was the first time in her life that she had ever been out of sight of other horses for more than a few minutes at a time, so now she was frightened and uneasy.

Her shrill whinnies brought no answer, and she trotted stiffly to the top of the nearest low ridge to look about and call again. But still she heard no answer, nor saw any sign of the other horses.

So for a while she grazed, moving restlessly from one small patch of green grass to another. And after a time, the worst of her hunger taken care of, she started slowly back the way she'd come the day before.

In her panic, the filly had not run in a straight line after escaping from the horse hunters. Instead, she'd blundered blindly down crooked canyons that turned and twisted—and on the flats, when she was forced to turn aside by a butte or washout in her path, she'd continued to run in the new direction until some new obstacle forced her to turn aside again.

Although she'd run a long way in this zigzag fashion, she was still no great distance from the place where the other wild horses had been trapped. But she was stiff and sore from the long

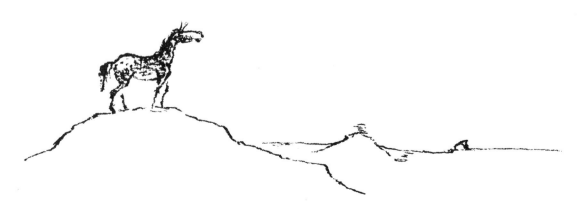

run and bruised by the falls she'd taken, so now she moved slowly. And instead of going as directly as possible back to where she'd last seen the others, she traveled a roundabout way, from one bit of high ground to the next.

She'd break into a trot, making soft whickering sounds to herself, before reaching the top of each knoll or ridge, then stand looking hopefully about for the other horses. But no matter how carefully she examined the country around her, she saw no sign of movement anywhere.

So it was the middle of the day when the filly came out onto the top of the ridge overlooking the little valley she'd escaped from the day before. She'd hesitated a long time, making many false starts, then turning back, before finally climbing this last ridge.

But she'd heard no sound of the plane, and at last had gone cautiously up the trail to stand on the highest part. For a long time she stood there, shifting her feet uneasily and snorting softly, but the little valley was empty. She saw no move-

ment anywhere, or heard any sound except the big flies buzzing in the grass.

So at last she started down into the place, but had taken only a few steps when she snorted in fear and whirled back as an airplane-shaped thing suddenly appeared in the air directly in front of her.

It was only a great golden eagle soaring with motionless wings on an updraft of warm air from the floor of the valley below. But the filly didn't stop for a second look as she scrambled back over the ridge top and down the other side. She'd run some distance before her first panic passed, and she stopped to look around.

The eagle, still silently wheeling higher and higher, was now only a tiny speck in the sky. And she'd heard no airplane sound, so after a time she climbed back up the ridge and went down the other side.

She wandered about over the little flat, whinnying again and again and sniffing the ground along the crisscrossing stock paths. But there was still no answer to her calling, and the heavy rain the night before had washed away all tracks and scent of the wild horses as well as those ridden by the horse hunters.

Finding no sign of the others, she grazed uneasily for a while. Then late in the afternoon she left the valley, following the same canyon trail the horse hunters had used when they drove the captured horses away the day before.

But here too the rain had washed away all tracks and scent, so when she came out of the canyon, the filly left the trail and drank from a pool of rainwater among the rocks before going off to graze. At dusk she moved into a little draw out of the cold night wind, and settled down uneasily for the night.

6

FOR SEVERAL DAYS the Appaloosa filly wandered disconsolately through the nearby canyons and over the ridges on either side of the little valley where she'd last seen the rest of the wild horses. She regularly interrupted her grazing to stand looking around from nearby high places, and whinnying for the others.

Unused to being alone, she was fearful and nervous, snorting and starting at any sudden sound or movement. A grouse whirring out from under her feet or a rabbit moving into the sunlight from the shade of a bush nearby would set her to trembling with fear. Even the rustling sounds of the deer mice and other small creatures searching the leaves under nearby thickets of buckbrush kept her wakeful and uneasy in the night.

The late spring grass was getting better, and the filly was able to find rainwater in dozens of little potholes among the rocks, so for a while she didn't wander far from the canyon's mouth. But no more rain fell, and when the first hot winds began to blow, these places dried up, one by one.

So late one afternoon, driven by thirst, she started down a stock trail the wild horses had often used when going to water. The old path wound its way along the sides of steep slopes, across small flats, and in one place it ran between the high walls of a narrow canyon. The filly hesitated a long time before entering this dark shadowy place alone, although she'd had no fear of it when she'd come this way with the other horses.

But the need to drink drove her on, and at the other end the path led her around and between strange water and wind-worn buttes, and finally to the top of a low ridge. From the top she could see the familiar water hole.

For a long time she stood uneasily sniffing the air and watching the flat beyond. A flock of sage grouse on their way to water walked single file along the path ahead of her, clucking softly to themselves. And a mule deer doe just leaving the water nuzzled her fawn behind her, then stood with her head up and big ears spread wide, looking toward the horse.

But except for these the filly could see no sign of movement anywhere. So after watching a little longer, while the doe with her fawn close behind her moved unhurriedly off, the Appaloosa walked cautiously ahead. Sniffing the muddy edges of the little pool, she caught no scent of horses—only the tracks of the deer and the scribbly footprints of the grouse and other birds.

After she'd finished drinking, she went by another of the many paths radiating out from the

water hole to find grass further back among the high ridges.

As the days passed, the lonely filly found patches of good grass almost everywhere. Except for her daily trips to water, she still stayed among the high peaks and ridges near the little valley where she'd last seen her mother and the other horses of the wild band.

In the cool mornings, she grazed along the bottoms of the canyons or on the lower slopes of the ridges. But during the hot middle of the day, she'd climb to the top of some nearby hill or knoll where there was almost always a little updraft from the slopes below to keep the biting flies away.

There she would drowse, idly switching her tail, until the late afternoon shadows brought shade again to the canyon bottoms. Then she would stretch, shake herself, and move down one or another of the old stock paths leading to one of the water holes in the lower hills.

The Appaloosa never found any sign of other horses when she sniffed around the muddy edges of the water hole, but the old mule deer and her fawn often came to the water at the same time she did. The deer paid little attention to the filly and after drinking, usually spent some time idling on the flat nearby before going on about her business.

The filly seemed to enjoy the company of the deer, and would watch interestedly as the fawn suckled or had its coat groomed by the doe. Sometimes it would be early dusk before the doe finally roused her fawn and moved off to wherever she would spend the night, while the filly turned back towards the high peaks.

Later, the weather changed and there came a time when every afternoon huge thunderheads began piling up in the sky in the West. The wild filly paid little attention to ordinary rain, simply humping her back and standing patiently with her head down and rump to the wind until it had passed. But when these dark clouds towered higher and higher, and she heard the first faint rumbles of far-off thunder, she would move un-

easily down from the higher ridges to some more sheltered place. Uneasy as she was, when the storm came closer, some change in the air and the crackle of electricity in her mane seemed to excite her. Without warning she'd suddenly leave off her grazing to gallop about, wheeling and turning this way and that, and snorting in playful fashion through widened nostrils.

Soon, however, the sky would turn dark and gusts of cold wind would spring up, just ahead of the rain and the almost continuous flashes of lightning and peal after peal of thunder that echoed back and forth from ridge to ridge.

And at the first big drops of rain, the filly would take what shelter she could find against some overhanging cliff or in some plum or chokecherry thicket. Drenched by the cold, beating rain and frightened by the lightning and thunder, she'd stand shivering and snorting softly to herself until the storm had passed.

During one such storm, she had taken shelter in the head of a little box canyon. Standing in a shallow, scooped-out depression at the base of one wall, the cliffs on either side protected her from the wind while an overhanging ledge above kept off most of the rain. And for a while she was comparatively dry and comfortable.

But then a small stream of muddy water began to trickle down from the edge of the cliff overhead, soon making an ankle-deep pool around her feet, and she pushed back closer to the rock wall behind her, but wasn't much alarmed.

The roll of thunder and flashing of lightning were almost continuous—and the wind blew in great gusts over the ridges. Then after an especially bright flash of lightning, there was a great crash from the ridge above as a long-dead tree was blown down by the wind.

As it fell, its roots were torn out of the ground, dislodging a mass of rocks and mud that started sliding downhill towards the canyon's edge. Gaining momentum as it went and loosening other rocks in its path, the slide was moving at express train speed by the time it shot over the edge of the cliff above where the filly stood.

Falling in a great arc, the old tree and the rocks behind it crashed onto the canyon floor some distance out from the base of the cliff. The tree trunk was soon buried, the rocks bounced and rolled off the growing pile, but the overhanging ledge protected the filly, and she wasn't touched.

A few trickles of gravel and small rocks continued to fall after the main part of the slide had fallen, then even those dwindled to nothing. The storm passed as quickly as it had come, and as the filly carefully picked her way around piles of mud and rocks, the sun came out again. Except for some splashes of mud on her coat, she was none the worse for her experience as she left the canyon and went back to her interrupted grazing.

7

As SUMMER came on, the hot winds began to blow day after day across the Badlands. The grass on the higher ridges turned brown, and one by one the smaller water holes dried up, so that each day the Appaloosa filly had to travel longer and longer distances to find new places to drink.

She was growing rapidly and her new summer coat was sleek and shiny. It was too early in the year for the cockleburrs to have ripened, so although her mane and tail were growing long, they were still free of the usual wild horse mats and tangles. With her unusual markings, long legs and easy movements, she was developing into a strikingly handsome horse.

The little filly now spent less and less of her time whinnying and calling for the other horses. But she took a great interest in all of the small animals she came across in her wanderings. She spent part of a morning watching from a little distance as a coyote searched the high grass for mice and grasshoppers. And when the coyote trotted off to investigate a nearby colony of prairie dogs, she grazed quietly in the same direction.

Without planning to, she became a sort of partner in his hunting. Being much larger than the coyote, she was also much more visible. So while the prairie dogs scurried excitedly from den mound to den mound, or stood high on their hind legs to bark at her, they didn't notice the coyote going quietly about his business nearby.

When the whole noisy colony's attention was on the little Appaloosa, the coyote, ears folded

back and his belly close to the ground, was able to creep unnoticed from one small clump of sagebrush to another. Finally he had worked his way to within a few feet of a fat old prairie dog standing by his burrow entrance, barking frantically at the horse.

A prairie dog's burrow drops straight down for the first couple of feet, like a tiny well, and it is almost impossible for even the fastest attacker to snatch him off his mound before he tumbles out of reach. So the coyote waited, flattened motionless in the grass.

And at last the excited prairie dog, without bothering to look behind him, left his doorway and started running for another mound nearby for a better view of the filly. As soon as the prairie dog was well away from his burrow, the coyote made a quick rush, snapped him up and trotted away to eat his breakfast in a nearby thicket of buckbrush.

The filly grazed a while longer around the edge of the prairie dog settlement and finally wandered away, over a nearby ridge.

A few mornings later, just as she was starting her day's grazing, she heard the sound again—the same faint, far-off drone that had made the older horses so uneasy in the spring. Snorting and trembling, she threw up her head, trying to locate its source. As before, the strange buzzing grew louder and fainter by turns, but as she listened it seemed to be coming slowly nearer.

So after turning this way and that, shifting her feet nervously as she tried to find where the disturbing sound was coming from, she suddenly broke into a run and disappeared down a path leading into a network of brush-filled gullies and washouts at the bottom of the slope.

The man in the plane had hoped to find the filly, but even when he circled directly overhead, she stayed safely hidden by early morning shadows among the thick clumps of buffalo berry and wild plum bushes below. So after a time he gave up the search and flew away.

The filly didn't leave the protection of the thickets until late afternoon, when it was time to start the long walk to water. And when she'd finished drinking she didn't return to the high ridges as she usually did, but moved off in another direction.

In the days that followed, the Appaloosa drifted restlessly from place to place, searching for grass and water as well as for some sign of the other horses. And little by little, she worked her way down from the high ridges and into a lower part of the Badlands she'd never seen before.

One day, when the sun was high overhead, she found a patch of shade beside a little cutbank and settled down to doze the hot hours away. It was late afternoon before she stirred again. Then, smelling water somewhere in the distance, she started along a stock path leading in that direction.

She'd gone a mile or so when, rounding the shoulder of a black butte, she saw a small bunch of range cows and calves ahead of her. Whickering softly, she trotted to catch up with them. The cattle, strung out along the path, were also on their way to water and paid no attention as

she fell in at the end of the line.

When they reached the water hole and gathered around the edges to drink, the Appaloosa moved in among them and drank at the same time.

After they'd watered, the cows scattered out to graze, and the filly grazed quietly among them. And when a new calf, at some clumsy play, blundered against her legs, she reached down to nuzzle it and snuff softly at its shiny coat. The cattle grazed until dusk, and when they finally moved off to their bed ground, the Appaloosa followed along.

For several days she stayed with the little herd, sleeping on their bed ground, grazing with them during the day, and taking her place in the line when they went to water every afternoon. But after a while, she became restless again, and sometimes wandered away for a day or two at a time.

8

ON ANOTHER DAY, while the filly was on one of her lonely exploring trips away from the cattle, she came in sight of the river for the first time. The stream here ran in a wide loop around the edge of the Badlands, and on the far side, between the river and the scattered ranches beyond, were ranges of low hills covered with good grass.

At this time of year, the wide riverbed was nearly dry, with only a small trickle of water running between the exposed sandbars. The

filly, used to the canyons and narrow valleys behind her, seemed uneasy in these wider open
spaces. But by sundown she was thirsty, and at
last went cautiously out across the dry sandbars,
past a brushy hummock that in the wet season
was a small island, and drank at the tiny stream
beyond.

At the upstream end of the island, a great pile
of driftwood and trash from old floods had
lodged against a few stunted cottonwoods that
grew there. The trees and the few scattered
thickets of low bushes seemed to offer some shelter from the rising night wind, so when she had
finished drinking, the filly climbed the low bank
and cropped for a while at the clumps of grass
growing in the little clearings.

Late in the afternoon, the sky in the West had
turned dark, and from time to time the Appaloosa filly had heard far-off rumblings of thunder. But even now there was still no smell of rain
on the little wind blowing her way from the
Badlands, and when she'd finished her grazing,
she settled down among the cottonwoods and
went to sleep, undisturbed by the distant storm.

It was some time in the darkest part of the night when she was awakened by a small vibration of the ground beneath her feet that sent strange tinglings up her legs. Snorting and shifting her feet uneasily, she threw up her head to listen, and felt rather than heard a low roaring sound coming from somewhere far off.

But no matter which way she turned, she was unable to locate its source—it seemed to come from the air all around her. As the muffled sound grew louder, the strange shaking of the ground under her feet increased, and she started a time or two to leave the little island. However, each time she hesitated, just before stepping down into the dry channel, and turned back to the shelter of the cottonwoods.

Then, its roaring seeming to shake the air, a great wall of water swept around the bend of the dry riverbed from upstream, rolling a great windrow of trash and driftwood ahead of it. Even in the dark the filly could see the pale streak of foam along its top edge, and the shadowy shapes of uprooted trees tumbling end over end towards her.

The thunder the filly had heard in the afternoon was from a storm that had brought a cloudburst to the hills at the head of the river, miles beyond the edge of the Badlands. The sudden downpour had sent sheets of water rushing down the slopes, quickly filling every gully and stream below to overflowing. Now the flood waters from a hundred streams were roaring down the dry riverbed towards the island where the filly stood snorting with fear.

The pile of old driftwood already lodged against the cottonwoods protected the filly from the first rush of water as it struck the head of the island and tumbled by on either side. But as the face of the flood passed downstream, the water behind it continued to rise, and in minutes the entire island was covered inches deep. The swirling of the rapidly rising water made it difficult for the filly to keep her footing. But she managed to brace herself against it until it was lapping around her flanks. Then a sudden eddy washed the ground from beneath her feet, and carried her away.

In the darkness she could only swim blindly with the current, trying to keep her head above water.

Carried first in one direction and then another by vicious crosscurrents and great swirling eddies that threatened to suck her beneath the surface, she somehow managed to avoid the huge "haystacks" where the flood water boiled over and around underwater obstructions. Fence posts floated by, trailing long pieces of barbwire that could have entangled her legs. And the branches of uprooted trees flailed the water on every side. But luckily none came close enough to do more than slightly bruise and scratch her.

At last, miles downstream, she was swept into a quiet backwater close to the bank and felt her feet touch bottom.

The filly was chilled and almost exhausted, but with the last of her strength she managed to wade, slipping and stumbling, into shallower water and scramble up the bank onto dry ground.

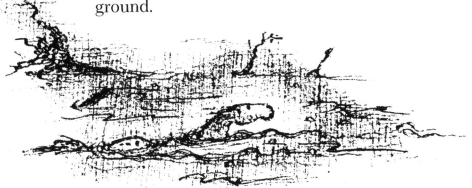

9

WHEN DAYLIGHT CAME, the little Appaloosa was standing on a small knoll some distance back from the riverbank. Her muddy coat had nearly dried, and excepting a few skinned places on her sides and legs, she seemed little the worse for her night's adventure.

When she raised her head to look about in the glowing light, she found that in the darkness the night before she had not only been carried a long way downstream—but across the river as well.

The main part of the flood had already passed, leaving a band of muddy silt and trash between the high-water mark and the water's edge. But even so, the river still ran almost bank full between her and the familiar Badlands on the other side.

For a while she cropped nervously at the grass around her feet, throwing up her head between bites to look across the river and whinny. When it was full light, she walked down slowly to sniff suspiciously at the line of trash piled along the high-water mark. Then after standing a while, whickering as she looked across the wide swift stream, she took a few cautious steps towards the river.

When she felt her feet begin to slide on the slippery slope, she whirled back to safer footing on the grass.

After she'd gotten over her fright, she wandered uneasily along the riverbank for a while, stopping often to whinny and look across to the Badlands. Later in the morning, she found a

DENVER
PUBLIC LIBRARY

FEB ͟ ͟ 1994

place where the slope was not so steep and was able to pick her way safely across the mud to stand at the water's edge.

For some time she stood there and watched the yellow water flowing by. Now and again an uprooted tree, tumbling and turning, floated down the middle of the stream, but otherwise nothing showed on the surface except the occasional boiling of the current.

And then, with her head low and nostrils wide to sniff the way, the filly stepped carefully into the water and started wading towards the other side.

The water was shallow at first, and she went ahead without difficulty. But after a few yards it suddenly deepened, and when she felt the swift current swirling against her sides, she panicked. Snorting in fear she turned back, plunging and splashing towards firmer ground. Losing her footing on the slippery bank she fell, but quickly scrambled to her feet and onto the dry grass again, where she stood trembling and shaking.

For most of the morning, the filly stayed close

to the riverbank, and several times at different places, she waded a little way into the river. But each time when she felt the water rising about her legs, she took fright and turned back.

So at last, when the sun was high overhead, she turned away from the river and drifted off towards the unfamiliar brown hills.

The country on this side of the river was quite different from the high, rough Badlands the filly had known before. Little draws with thickets of wild plum and chokecherry ran on easy slopes between the low rounded hills. There was good grass everywhere, and the water holes were all nearly full, so she no longer had to travel long distances each day to find either one.

With living so easy, the Appaloosa drifted here and there among the hills, growing fat and sleek, and spending long hours each day simply dozing in some pleasant place. She had been wandering aimlessly about this new range for a good many days when, late one afternoon, she turned aside to drink at a little spring seeping out from under the base of a black-shale cut-

bank, and found that other horses had been there not long before.

The mud all round the little pool had been trampled by many hooves, and the strong scent of horses still hung in the air. Making small excited whickering sounds and clearing her nostrils regularly, the filly snuffed and nuzzled at the fresh tracks. Then, standing with her head high, she whinnied shrilly, flicking her sharp, pointed ears back and forth, listening for an answer, and when none came she whinnied again. But still the only sound she heard was the usual bickering of magpies in the distance.

After turning back for a hurried drink at the pool, the filly trotted up the old stock path to the top of the nearby ridge. Dropping her head now and again as she climbed to sniff the trampled dust, she found scattered signs of the horses having gone this way. But when she reached the top and looked anxiously about, there was nothing to be seen anywhere but grass and sagebrush. And beyond where she stood, the dust in the path showed no tracks at all.

The horses she was following had turned off the path just beyond the crest of the ridge, and on the grass they left no trail she could follow.

So she too left the trail and went on, turning aside to look about from the top of every knoll and hill in the neighborhood. Sometimes walking, sometimes trotting, and stopping now and again to graze a while, she drifted aimlessly in a wide circle. But when full dark came, and the bullbats swooped about their business overhead, she still had not found the horses she was searching for.

Settling down for the night in a little draw, she slept fitfully, waking now and then to whinny hopefully for the strange horses. And at first light she started her search again.

It was the middle of the morning when from the top of a small hill she looked down and saw them—fifteen or twenty range horses—scattered over the flat below her.

These were the first horses the filly had seen since the day she'd been separated from the wild horse band, weeks before. She whinnied softly,

then started trotting towards them. Hearing her whinny, the strange horses raised their heads and turned to watch her as she came down the slope and stopped some distance off. Then all—except the old mare with a colt—turned unconcernedly back to their feeding.

The Appaloosa stood where she was for a bit, tossing her head, until the mare, leaving her colt behind, started walking towards her. Coming close, the mare cautiously stretched her neck to sniff the filly's muzzle. Then, not recognizing the stranger's scent, she laid her ears back, squealed, whirled, and let fly with both hind feet at the filly's ribs.

Avoiding the kick, the filly loped off a little way and turned again to watch as the mare went back to her colt and her interrupted grazing.

10

ALL DAY the filly stayed in the neighborhood of the strange horses, even though one or another of the older mares would lay her ears back, snap her teeth, and make a threatening run towards her whenever she came too close.

And in the late afternoon when the others strung out on the way to water, the filly followed them at a distance. She stopped and waited until the others had watered and moved off to graze before she went for her own drink.

For several days this went on. However, after a time, the range horses began to lose their distrust of the stranger and finally allowed her to graze among them without interference. On the daily trips to water she took her place in line, and joined in the crowding as they drank. The mares made no objection now when she nuzzled a colt or joined the other yearlings in their mock fights or sudden spurts of racing about.

And one hot afternoon when the horses were drowsing on a high hilltop, standing in pairs head to tail to switch flies off themselves and each other, she moved cautiously up beside an old speckled gray mare standing alone. The mare took no notice except to rub her head against the filly's flank to dislodge a troublesome fly from her own forehead, and for the rest of the afternoon they drowsed there, side by side.

She had been with the range horses for a couple of weeks or so when she looked up from her grazing one afternoon and saw a rider skylined on a ridge not far off. He simply sat on his horse

there for a few minutes, then turned and rode out of sight.

The other horses had thrown up their heads to look, and when the man came no closer, they went back to their feeding. But at the first sight of him, the Appaloosa had whirled and galloped frantically in the opposite direction.

She didn't stop until she was a mile or more away, and it wasn't until morning that she came back by roundabout ways to where the other horses were grazing. And even then she watched from a distance for a long time, making sure there were no riders in sight, before she finally took her place among them.

11

WHEN BERT rode into the ranch late that afternoon, he found Torwal watering his horse at the windmill trough.

Getting down off his own horse, Bert said, "I saw the wild Appaloosa today. She was with a bunch of our horses over by the Cedar Springs!" He tried to sound matter of fact, but in spite of himself his voice went high from excitement.

"Are you sure it was the wild one you saw?" Torwal asked.

"I got a good look at her," Bert told him, "and she's the one all right. The purtiest horse you ever saw."

"An Appaloosa filly, eh?" Torwal answered. "It doesn't seem likely there'd be two of them. But how in the world do you suppose she got mixed up with our horses, anyway?"

"I told you she was smart and could look out for herself," Bert answered. "Couldn't we go out and drive her in with the other horses?"

Torwal thought a while, then said, "If she's the one those fellows saw—and the way she quit the bunch when you showed up makes it look possible—she's wild as an antelope.

"You try to bring her in now," he went on, "you'll only spook her and she'll leave the country."

"But she's so purty, somebody else may try to catch her," Bert answered. "And I bet if we just had her here in the pasture a while she'd get tame real quick!"

"If I was you and felt like that about her," Torwal said, "I'd ride out and look at that bunch every day or two, but not stop or go close. Maybe after a while she'll get used to seeing you and not head for the hills every time you show up.

"Those springs will be drying up before long," he went on, "and we'll have to start leaving the gates open so the horses can come to the wind-mill for water. Maybe she might follow them in."

"Yeah," Bert agreed, enthusiastically, "then later when we shut them in for the winter, she'd be with them and it wouldn't be any trouble at all to get her tame!"

"Might be," Torwal said. "Anyway, it's worth thinking about. Now let's get about our chores."

12

WHEN SHE'D finally rejoined the other horses after her fright at seeing Bert the day before, the filly was still nervous and uneasy, constantly interrupting her feeding to throw up her head and look carefully at the skyline all round.

And a few days later she saw him again. He was a long distance off and not coming in her direction, but even so she quickly left the others to their grazing and disappeared among the hills behind her. And as she'd done before, she stayed hidden in the rough country all through the night before returning to the bunch.

During the following weeks, Bert rode out every few days to look for the filly. At first she always left the others and disappeared as soon as he came in sight. But as time went on, finding that this horseman never came close or seemed to take any interest in her, she began to lose some of her uneasiness.

So instead of disappearing and not coming back for hours, she'd simply move off a hundred yards or so, then stand watching until he'd gone out of sight before going back to her grazing.

And even on the day she saw two riders appear, instead of one, she only moved off a little farther than usual before turning to watch them as they stopped their horses for a few minutes on a nearby hill.

On this particular day Torwal had ridden along with Bert to get a look at the wild filly himself. So now he took an old pair of field glasses out of his saddlebag and looked carefully at the little Appaloosa standing some way be-

yond the grazing range horses.

"I think you're right," he said after a bit. "That must be the one that got away from the wild bunch. But how do you suppose she got out of the Badlands and onto this side of the river?"

"I dunno," Bert answered. "But that's the one those fellows were after, all right. And isn't she a purty thing, just like I said?"

"She'll make somebody a real fancy saddle horse when she gets her growth," Torwal agreed. "And you notice she doesn't quit the bunch when you show up now?

"It just might be that she'll follow the others when we bring them into the pasture in the fall," he went on. "If she does that you'll have all winter to get her used to you."

"Yessir!" Bert agreed. "I think she's already getting to know me a little, and by spring I bet I can start halterbreaking her!"

"Might be," Torwal agreed, "but let's move on now before we spook her again."

13

Towards the end of the summer, the water holes and springs out on the open range began to dry up, and one morning Torwal said to Bert after breakfast, "I think it's time we brought those horses in so they can begin watering here at the windmill."

"Maybe we can bring the wild filly along with them," Bert exclaimed.

"I don't know about that," Torwal answered as he finished saddling his horse, "but we'll see how she acts."

They rode out of the big pasture, leaving the gate open behind them, and finally found the range horses grazing not far from the dried-up Cedar Springs. These horses were unbroken and wild in their way, but they were used to being driven from place to place by mounted men. So now, as Torwal and Bert circled quietly to come up behind them, they bunched up and started in the direction of the ranch.

As soon as Torwal and Bert had come in sight, the Appaloosa filly had left the others and moved some distance off, then turned to stand watching. But when they started directly towards the grazing horses, she became uneasy and galloped out of sight down a nearby draw.

"Look!" Bert exclaimed. "She's going to get away! Can't we head her off?"

"No," Torwal answered, "we'd only spook her clean out of the country."

"But we'll lose her," the boy insisted.

"Maybe so," the man replied, "but she's friendly with these horses now, and I think she'll not go far."

"You really think she won't go back to the Badlands?" Bert asked, anxiously.

"I'm pretty certain," Torwal replied. And after a little bit he spoke again. "Look, boy," he said. "Over on that ridge to your right!"

The boy looked in the direction he was pointing and saw the filly watching them from a low ridge a half a mile away.

"You see," Torwal remarked, "she hasn't left the country after all. I think she'll stay out of sight most of the time, but she'll follow along to see where these horses are going."

So the man and the boy went on about their business, driving the bunch slowly towards the ranch. They saw the filly once or twice more during the morning, watching from far off, but she never came close.

The open pasture gate was built of heavy planks and hinged to two tall posts connected by a crossbar at the top. But the range horses went through without hesitation and trotted down the deep worn stock path to the water troughs by the clanking windmill. Torwal and Bert waited until they'd all watered, then drove them back through the gate and out onto the range again.

"We'll leave the gate open," Torwal said. "And now that they know about the water they'll come in every afternoon to drink."

"But what about the filly?" Bert wanted to know.

"She's waiting for them out there now, is my bet," Torwal said. "And one of these days she'll follow them in if we just give her time."

"I hope you're right," Bert said, doubtfully.

"I'd bet on it," Torwal told him as they turned and rode back to the ranch.

When the range horses had gone out through the gate and drifted back into the hills to graze, they found the little Appaloosa watching for them from a ridge a mile or so away. After making sure there were no riders following them, she finally trotted in their direction. She touched noses with two or three of the other yearlings, then settled down to graze, close to the old speckled gray mare.

And the next afternoon, when the others

started back towards the ranch for water, she went along with them as far as the ridge overlooking the pasture gate and the windmill below. But at the sound of the clanking iron pump rods and the whirring of the windmill blades, she snorted and turned back the way she'd come, to look for water elsewhere.

Most of the springs and water holes on the range were already dry, but she was still able to find a few wet places where a little water seeped into small puddles and old horse tracks. She seldom found enough for a real drink, but for a while she seemed to manage well enough. And each afternoon, when the range horses turned towards the ranch, she followed them until they came in sight of the gate.

The horses came in for water at about the same time every day, and Bert always arranged his chores so that he could be on top of the little hill behind the ranch house with Torwal's field glasses when they came in sight—hoping to see the filly follow the others in.

For the first few days she turned back and dis-

appeared from sight as soon as she saw the gate. Later, seeming to have lost some of her uneasiness, she would simply stop on top of the ridge and wait while the others went on down to the troughs to drink. When they'd finished and drifted back out of the pasture she'd trot up to them, touch muzzles with one or two, then follow them back out onto the range. But still she made no move to come through the gate.

Bert was becoming more and more discouraged, for it looked as if the filly was never going to come inside the fence.

"Give her time, boy," Torwal told him when Bert suggested that maybe they should try to catch her on the range after all. "Almost all the water holes out there are dried up by now," he went on. "And if nothing spooks her, she'll be back when she's ready."

"Maybe so," Bert agreed, doubtfully, "but what if she goes back to the Badlands? We'd never find her again. Besides, as long as she's running loose out on the range, somebody else may catch her."

"Even if they do see her," Torwal assured him, "they'll have a hard time catching her. And if we don't spook her, she'll come in when she gets thirsty enough.

"And when she does,". he added, "she'll soon get used to the place. Then one day we'll close the gate and shut her in the pasture with the others for the winter."

Bert wasn't convinced, but discouraged as he was he still lay flat in the grass on the hilltop every afternoon, watching and hoping.

The dry weather held on, and the small seeps dried up, one by one, until at last the filly was unable to find water anywhere. And one afternoon, when she'd been without water for three days, she stayed behind as usual when the other horses started through the gate. There was no wind, for once, so the clanking pump rods were still. While Bert watched she stood a while sniffing the smell of water from the overflowing tanks. Then when the others started trotting towards the windmill, she tossed her head a time or two, making little whickering sounds to her-

self, and suddenly galloped after them.

The range horses were already drinking when she caught up with them, but she was suspicious of the strange troughs and nosed the trampled mud around the overflow instead. However, she found only thin mud there in the horse tracks. So, finally her thirst overcame her fear and she crowded in beside the old gray mare and plunged her muzzle greedily into the cold water.

Seeing the filly drinking there at last, Bert was already planning how he would go about getting her over her wildness once she was safely shut in the pasture with the other horses. Then a sudden gust of wind set the windmill turning. At the first clank of the pump rods the Appaloosa whirled and ran back up the trail. For a moment Bert thought she was going to crash into the barbwire fence, but she went safely through the gate and was soon out of sight.

The boy lay on the hill after the Appaloosa had disappeared. It looked as if his dream of taming the wild filly was gone for good. After a

while he walked slowly down to the ranch house to where Torwal sat on the steps fixing a hacka-more.

"Did the filly come down to the windmill with the others today?" he asked.

"Yeah," Bert answered, without enthusiasm.

"Good!" Torwal said. "I sort of figured she might."

"Trouble is," Bert told him, "she went right back out, on a dead run."

And he told Torwal about the filly's fright at the windmill, and of how near she came to running into the wire fence.

"She acted plumb scared out of her wits," he went on, "and the way she was running she probably won't stop until she's clear back in the Badlands—and I'll never see her again!"

Torwal went on with his work for a while, then spoke up again. "Too bad," he said, at last. "But I wouldn't give up yet, if I was you. That wild filly has thrown in with this bunch, and no horse likes to be alone, so I don't think she'll go far. Besides, she got a taste of the water."

"Maybe so," Bet answered, doubtfully. "But if you'd seen the way she was running . . ."

"Well," Torwal pointed out, "she must have been pretty badly spooked by the airplane business, from what they said, and the windmill took her by surprise. But I still think she'll be back, and when she sees the other horses pay no attention to the noise, she'll get over her scare."

They sat for a while, then Torwal spoke again. "Just give her time, boy," he said as he got to his feet. "Just give her time and everything will turn out all right."

Bert didn't seem convinced, but he said nothing more.

The next day, he watched anxiously until he saw the filly come over the ridge with the range horses, as usual.

There was a brisk wind blowing, so the windmill was clanking steadily. Hearing the sound, she hesitated a while before following the others

through the gate. But after some listening and sniffing she came cautiously down the slope for a way, then stood again facing the windmill with her head up and nostrils wide.

And when the range horses went on drinking, paying no attention to the strange noises, she finally pushed her way among them and snatched a quick drink before whirling away.

After a few days she seemed to lose her fear of the noisy windmill, and no longer paid it any mind.

"You were right," Bert remarked one night as he and Torwal were getting supper. "The filly comes in for water every afternoon now, and doesn't seem to be afraid of the windmill anymore."

"I thought she would," Torwal answered. "Next week we'll close the gate and turn them all into the big pasture for the winter."

"Then she'll be ours!" the boy exclaimed. "Nobody can get her out of there!"

"That's right," Torwal assured him. "She'll be

all yours. She's lost a lot of her wildness already, and in the pasture she'll lose a lot more."

And from then on, as Bert did his chores, he planned the way he'd go about taming the Appaloosa filly. He wondered if maybe he could ride her in the Fourth-of-July parade next summer. He thought about how the people would talk and point him out when they saw him riding a wild Appaloosa he'd caught and tamed himself.

The Appaloosa spent much of her time during the first days in the big pasture walking along the fences looking for a way out. And when Torwal and Bert rode through on one errand or another, she'd back into the farthest fence corner and stand watching uneasily until they'd gone out of sight. But after a time she settled down and would only raise her head, like the others, when a rider went by, then return to her grazing.

14

WORD SOON spread that Torwal and Bert had
found the wild Appaloosa with a bunch of their
range horses and had her in their pasture. Almost every day a neighbor or two dropped by to
admire her—and to wonder how she'd gotten
from the Badlands to this side of the river. They
called Bert a lucky fellow and asked him about
his plans for making her into a saddle horse.

But one day two of the wild horse hunters
rode in, and they were not altogether pleased.

76

"I hear you've got our wild Appaloosa here," the leader said to Torwal first off.

"I don't know about her being yours," Torwal answered him, "but there she is, over by the windmill."

"That's the one, all right," the leader said to his partner.

"She got away from us when we trapped that wild bunch over in the Badlands," he went on. "And if it's all right with you, we'll catch her up right now and thank you for holding her for us."

Bert listened without saying anything. But Torwal didn't seem much concerned. "I don't think that would be right," he said. "From what I heard you never did catch her, so she was never yours."

"But she was the one we were really after when we cleaned out that wild bunch," the leader objected. "It's just that somehow she got away when we was running the others into the trap."

"That was months ago," Torwal pointed out. "If you wanted her so badly, you had plenty of

time to go back in there and bring her out before this.

"Some way or other she got clear over here and took up with our horses," he went on. "She's a 'slick'—no brand on her—and we brought her in with the others."

"It don't seem right," the leader complained. "We chased her all through those Badlands, and now you claim she belongs to you instead of us.

"And if we have to," he threatened, "we can come over here some night and get her, being as she really belongs to us."

Torwal still seemed unconcerned as he said, "In the first place, friend, you said yourself that you chased her all over those hills but never got a rope on her. And besides, the whole country knows that horse now, and how she happens to be in our pasture."

The horse hunters were not happy about the way things had turned out, but finally they left, muttering to themselves.

"Do you think they'll really come back and

try to get her?" Bert asked as the men rode away.

"No," Torwal assured him. "Like I told the fellow, she got away when he trapped the others in the Badlands, and he didn't go back and try to catch her later on, so she's all yours."

"I'm glad of that," Bert answered. "She's such a purty thing, I couldn't have stood losing her."

"Don't worry about it," Torwal told him. "Now let's go fix some fence. I saw some loose wire over on the west side yesterday, and we wouldn't want that filly to get out now."

"No sir," the boy agreed. And all morning as they worked on the fence, he thought what a fine thing it was going to be—owning the fanciest saddle horse in the country. Of course he'd have to tame her first, but he didn't think that would be very hard to do.

Also, he'd have to think up a name for her— he couldn't go on just calling her "the filly" or "the Appaloosa." Any way you looked at it, he was going to have a busy winter!